For Lina, who shows me how to dig deep.
For Lee and Lindsay, who gave me roots.
And for Abigail, who sees the forest for the trees.

For my family and the forest,
who have both given me so much.

Random House Studio with colophon is a trademark of Penguin Random House LLC.

Visit us on the Web! rhcbooks.com

Educators and librarians, for a variety of teaching tools, visit us at RHTeachersLibrarians.com

Library of Congress Cataloging-in-Publication Data is available upon request.
ISBN 978-0-593-38014-7 (trade) — ISBN 978-0-593-38015-4 (lib. bdg.) — ISBN 978-0-593-38016-1 (ebook)

The illustrations were rendered digitally.

MANUFACTURED IN CHINA
10 9 8 7 6 5 4 3 2 1
First Edition

once upon
a forest

PAM FONG

RANDOM HOUSE STUDIO
NEW YORK

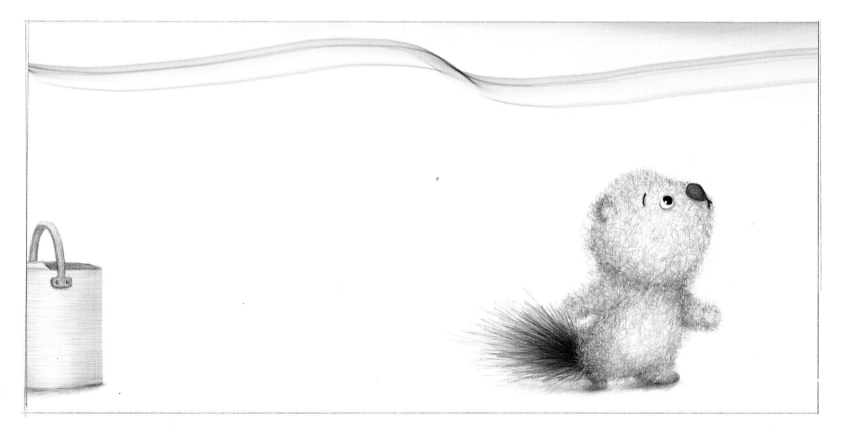

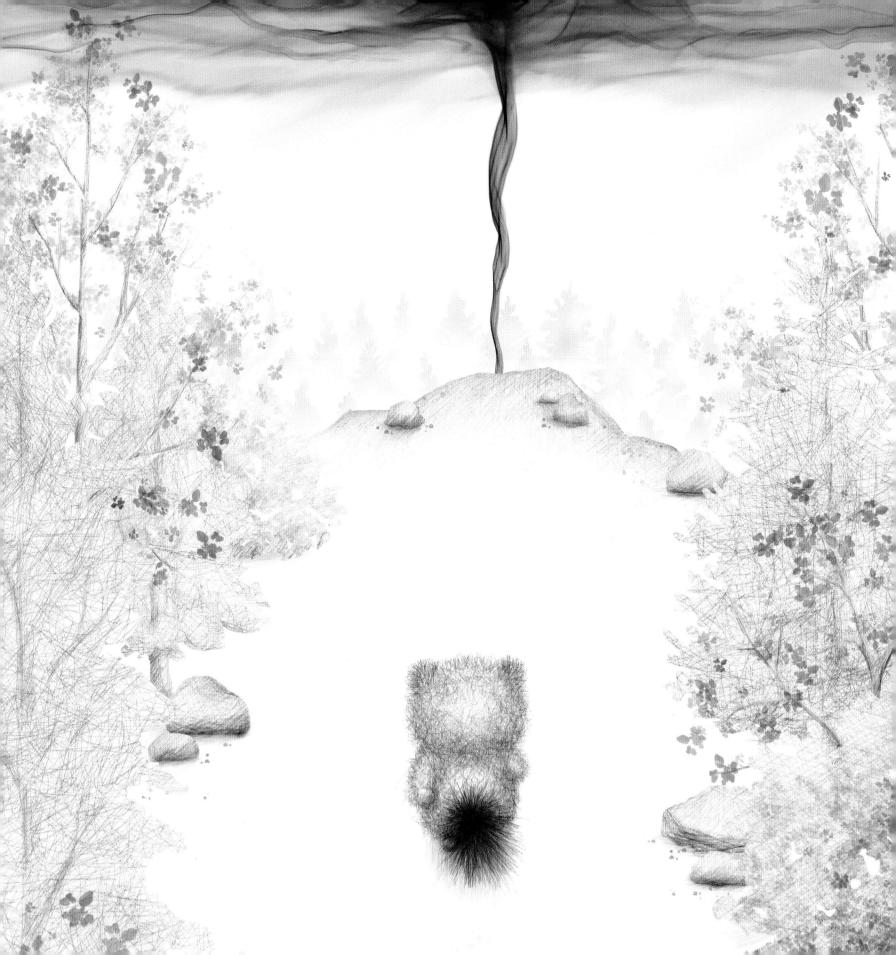

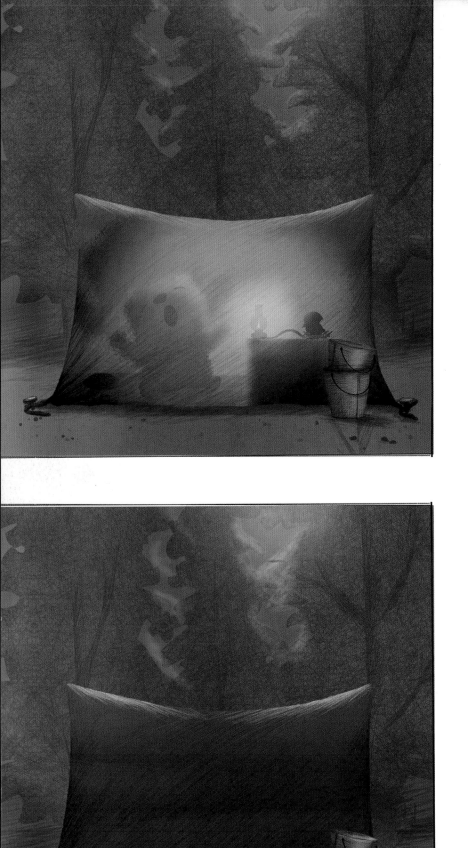

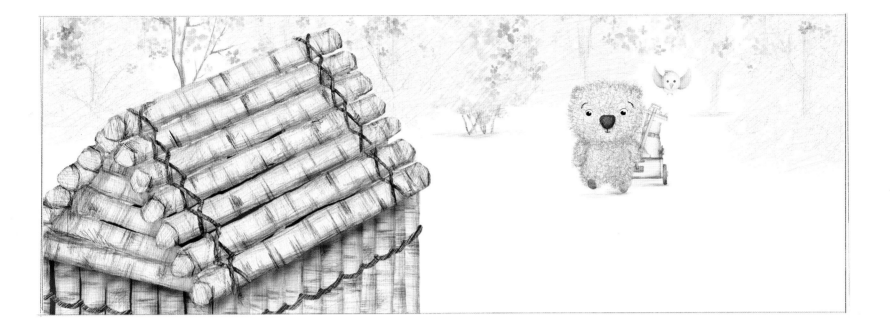